LAND OF MOUNTAINS AND ISLANDS

Because of the many bays and inlets along its coastline, only a small part of Greece is more than fifty miles from the sea. Three-fourths of the mainland is covered by mountains. The highest mountain is Mount Olympus, mythological home of the Greek gods. Where the mountain ranges extend into the surrounding seas, their peaks form thousands of islands that account for almost one-fifth of the land area of Greece.

THE PELOPONNESE

Plato's story takes place in the Peloponnese, the most southerly region of mainland Greece. The Peloponnese was once a peninsula, joined to the rest of the mainland by the Isthmus of Corinth. A four-mile-long canal across the Isthmus was completed in 1893, so the Peloponnese is now technically an island. The Peloponnese is famous for its beauty and its many ancient ruins.

MODERN GREECE

On small family farms, a third of the Greek people grow grains, cotton, tobacco, potatoes, melons, tomatoes, grapes, citrus fruit, and olives. Goats are raised for milk and sheep for meat. Most of the rest of the population is concentrated in a few cities, a fourth in the area of Athens, the capital. Many Greek people make their living from the sea — in the fishing, shipping, and ship-building industries. Tourism is also an important part of the economy. Tourists are drawn by the ancient ruins throughout the country and by the beauty and mild climate of the Greek islands.

OLYMPIA TODAY

In 393 A.D. the festival at Olympia was banned by the Roman emperor Theodosius I. In the years that followed, foreign armies looted Olympia, earthquakes toppled its temples, and landslides and floods covered it with mud and sand. The history of Olympia was remembered, but its location was forgotten. Then, in the eighteenth century, Olympia was rediscovered. Archaeologists have now excavated the site, uncovering the remains of the great Temple of Zeus and other buildings. The stadium looks today much as it did when the footraces were run there, but only an arch remains of the vaulted tunnel through which the athletes made their entrance. In 1896, the games were revived through the efforts of Frenchman Pierre de Coubertin. The first modern-day Olympic Games were held that year in Athens.

PLATO'S JOURNEY

Written by Linda Talley

Illustrated by Itoko Maeno

MarshMedia, Kansas City, Missouri

To Bud — L.T.

For CAT — I.M.

Text ©1998 by Marsh Film Enterprises, Inc.

Illustrations ©1998 by Itoko Maeno

First Printing 1998
Second Printing 2000

Published by **MARSH**media
           A Division of Marsh Film Enterprises, Inc.
           P. O. Box 8082
           Shawnee Mission, KS 66208

Library of Congress Cataloging-in-Publication Data
Talley, Linda.
     Plato's journey/written by Linda Talley; illustrated by Itoko Maeno.
     p.   cm.
     Summary: After a series of lies told to him by other animals sends
Plato on a journey to Olympia to compete in a nonexistent goat race, he
returns hurt and humiliated. End pages provide information about
Greece and the Olympic games.
     ISBN 1-55942-100-2
     [1. Goats—Fiction. 2. Honesty—Fiction. 3. Greece—Fiction.]
I. Maeno, Itoko, ill. II. Title.
PZ7.T156355Pl 1998   97-13842
[E]—dc21

Book layout and typography by Cirrus Design

Printed in Hong Kong

Listen to a story about four falsehoods that led a goat named Plato on a journey he never forgot.

It all began the day Plato was stung by the bee. In an instant, he was careening down the stony hillside, through the olive grove, and into the farmyard of Madame Papanopoulos, where he nearly ran over his friend Demetri.

"Great Zeus!" laughed Demetri. "I have never in my life seen a goat move so quickly. You should be in the races!"

Plato was not amused.

But later, as he lay in the shade of a fig tree recovering from his bee sting, Plato reflected upon Demetri's words. A little smile settled across his face. "I never before realized I was capable of such extraordinary speed," Plato mused.

That afternoon Plato's friend Sophie was amazed to discover him tearing around the farmyard like a goat gone mad, running from the ancient olive tree at the edge of the grove, to the cypress tree at the corner of the farm, then pausing for a brief second to catch his breath before charging back the other way.

"Plato!" Sophie cried out in alarm. "Whatever are you doing?"

Plato trotted to her side, all out of breath and a bit wild eyed. "Sophie," he gasped, "I may have discovered a new talent. Have you ever seen a goat run so fast?"

Sophie, who was quite fond of Plato, did not know how to reply. She was younger by several years than Plato and believed that she herself could probably outrun him. Nevertheless, she did not want to hurt her friend's feelings.

"My dear," she said sweetly, "I am sure you are the fastest goat in all the Peloponnese."

Gregorios, another goat who lived on the farm, was listening to this conversation.

"What?" he called out. "Plato is the fastest goat in the Peloponnese?"

"So it seems," Plato replied.

Now Gregorios was very jealous of Plato. Plato had always been the favorite of Madame Papanopoulos, and around his neck he wore a beautiful bell she had given him. Gregorios had a notion how to make Plato look very foolish.

"I have an excellent idea!" Gregorios said. "The great goat race is being held this Saturday at Olympia. You must enter!"

"Olympia!" whispered Plato. It was a magic word, one he had heard spoken by the old people when they talked about the ancient times.

"Do you hear that, Sophie?" cried Plato. "I am certain I could win this race!"

Sophie had never heard of any goat race at Olympia, but she smiled encouragingly at Plato.

The next morning, while the dew was still on the olive leaves, Plato set
out on his journey.

"Adio!" called Sophie.

"Run your best race!" shouted Gregorios.

When he had traveled only a few kilometers, Plato met a rooster scratching by the side of the road. The rooster's name was Nikos. Plato explained that he was headed to Olympia to compete in Saturday's goat race.

"What a ridiculous goat," Nikos cackled to himself. "Still, I think I can profit from his ignorance."

"Ah, yes, the goat races," Nikos said. "How exciting. But where is your hat and where is your scarf? It is a great tradition that each goat in the race wears a hat and a scarf."

"But I have none," Plato wailed in despair. "I am certain to be disqualified!"

"Do not worry," comforted Nikos. "I have just the thing for you! Wait here!"

Off Nikos rushed to his chicken house. He dusted his wife off an old straw hat where she was roosting.

As he ran under his mistress' clothesline, he grabbed a brightly printed dish towel, then hurried back to Plato. "Here," he panted, tossing the towel around Plato's neck and pushing the hat over his ears.

Nikos took a step back and threw open his wings in a gesture of admiration. "Ah! You will be the handsomest goat at Olympia!"

But these were not gifts from the heart. Nikos had his eye on Plato's bell, picturing how handsome it would look against his own burnished feathers.

"All I ask in exchange for this fine hat and scarf is that old bell you have around your neck."

And so it was that Plato resumed his journey without his treasured bell. He missed its friendly sound, but he was consoled by thoughts of the great day to come. And that night, when he curled up under an olive tree to sleep, Plato dreamed it was his brow that wore the victory wreath and his name that sailed out over the grandstands when the winner was proclaimed.

Plato did not have far to go the next morning. As he crested a hill, he saw below, in the valley where the River Alpheus meets the River Cladeus, a grove of pine trees, and within the grove a forest of a different sort — a forest of stone columns. It was Olympia.

Plato could also see tiny colored
specks that he knew were people — come
to see the race, he thought with excitement.
"I'm on my way!" he called out. And half
trotting, half falling, he made his way down the
hill and over the bridge that crossed the river.

As Plato entered the grove, a woman was speaking to a small gathering of people.

"You are now in the Sacred Grove of Olympia," she said. "These great toppled columns are all that remain of the once magnificent Temple of Zeus."

Plato drew closer. But the speaker did not go on. It was then Plato realized that all eyes had turned from the speaker to him. Some of the people were smiling broadly, and he gave a goat smile back.

"Another tourist has joined our group," a man called out. "Good morning, Mr. Goat! I see you have dressed up in your finest clothes to visit the Temple of Zeus!" Now everyone was laughing out loud.

21

Quickly Plato made his escape, dodging the broken columns that littered the ground of the Sacred Grove. As he paused to collect himself, Plato looked up. He saw an arched entryway and knew at once that it led to the ancient stadium. Plato straightened his hat and scarf, then solemnly made his way under the arch.

When he came out into the stadium, Plato saw more people, but no signs of preparations for the race. "Where are the competitors?" he puzzled. At that moment, he heard a great flapping overhead.

Plato turned to see an eagle settle onto the nearby stones. The eagle turned his yellow eyes on Plato, studying him carefully.

"Are you like those foolish people in the Sacred Grove?" cried Plato. "Have you never before seen a goat properly dressed for the great goat race at Olympia?"

The eagle sighed. Then he spoke, not unkindly. "You have been deceived," he said. "Look about you, goat, at these ruins. There have been no races here for over a thousand years."

Suddenly Plato understood. His ears burned with embarrassment. Tears of humiliation stung his eyes. Quickly and quietly he made his way from Olympia.

On the road home, Plato came upon Nikos. "Nikos!" he cried as the rooster hid behind a shrub. "Yours was only one of the lies that led me on this journey. You could have told me there was no goat race, but you lied for your own profit — to gain my most treasured possession. Now I have only sadness to take back home."

26

Plato trudged on. As he neared his farm, he met Gregorios. "Gregorios," he said, "you knew there was no goat race at Olympia. You lied to me for no reason other than to make me look foolish. You succeeded."

As Plato came into the farmyard, he met Sophie. "Sophie," he sighed, "I know you were just trying to spare my feelings when you said I was the fastest goat in the Peloponnese. But it would have been kinder in the long run if you had just told me the truth — that I am fast enough and reliable enough to be Madame Papanopoulos' favorite goat, even if I might not be able to win any races."

At that moment, Demetri joined them.

"Ah, Demetri, my friend," said Plato, "what you said to me was false, but it was not a lie. You had no intention of deceiving me when you said you had never seen a goat run so fast. I foolishly deceived myself into thinking your simple pleasantry was meant seriously."

And so ended Plato's journey. Plato remembered it for his entire life and resolved that he would never, ever tell anyone a lie. He never did. And as the years went by, when people thought about Plato, they didn't remember his journey to Olympia at all.

But they did remember that Plato was the most honest goat
in all the Peloponnese!

Dear Parents and Educators:

Children tell lies for a variety of reasons. Between the ages of five and seven they typically fabricate stories and explanations as they learn to distinguish between reality and fantasy. In later years, children may lie because they feel trapped or threatened, or because they want to avoid embarrassment, punishment, or rejection. Sometimes children may think a lie will make things easier for themselves or for others. Children with low self-esteem may lie in the hopes of bolstering their standing with others.

And as much as we may want to instill honesty in our children, we may be sending some very mixed messages about the value of telling the truth. We reprimand children when they tell a lie, yet we may ask them to say we're napping when a neighbor drops by. We are appalled when a child fabricates a story to escape punishment, yet we may call in "sick" to work when we are actually quite well. Our children are quick to observe the inconsistencies between our admonitions and our behavior.

As adults we can encourage honesty in children by following these suggestions:

- Model honesty. Show children that you are willing to be truthful even when it requires a sacrifice.

- Reward honesty. Recognize children for their honest behaviors. Celebrate the effort it took to take that risk!

- Identify the feelings that accompany honesty. When people choose to be honest, they retain their self-respect. They don't have to be anxious about anyone discovering the "truth."

- Treat mistakes as learning opportunities and focus on solutions. Be a problem solver, not a blamer.

- Focus on building a close relationship of support and caring. Children who feel love and support are less likely to feel the need to lie. Children who care and empathize with others learn to be honest.

Plato's story can help children see the negative consequences that lying can produce. Use the following questions to help them understand the message of *Plato's Journey*.

- Why did Plato journey to Olympia?

- Who were the animals that encouraged Plato to make the journey?

- What did each one say to Plato? Did each animal have a reason for saying something that was not true?

- How did Plato feel when he returned to his home?

- What lesson did Plato learn?

- Did the other animals learn a lesson?

- Have you ever told a lie to a friend? What happened?

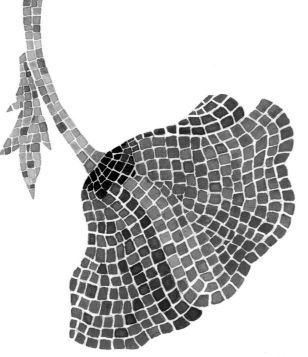

Available from MarshMedia

Storybooks — Hardcover with dust jacket and full-color illustrations throughout.

Videos — The original story and illustrations combined with dramatic narration, music, and sound effects.

Activity Books — Softcover collections of games, puzzles, maps, and project ideas designed for each title.

Amazing Mallika, written by Jami Parkison, illustrated by Itoko Maeno. 32 pages. ISBN 1-55942-087-1. Video. 15:05 run time. ISBN 1-55942-088-X.

Bailey's Birthday, written by Elizabeth Happy, illustrated by Andra Chase. 32 pages. ISBN 1-55942-059-6. Video. 18:00 run time. ISBN 1-55942-060-X.

Bea's Own Good, written by Linda Talley, illustrated by Andra Chase. 32 pages. ISBN 1-55942-092-8. Video. 15:00 run time. ISBN 1-55942-093-6.

Clarissa, written by Carol Talley, illustrated by Itoko Maeno. 32 pages. ISBN 1-55942-014-6. Video. 13:00 run time. ISBN 1-55942-023-5.

Gumbo Goes Downtown, written by Carol Talley, illustrated by Itoko Maeno. 32 pages. ISBN 1-55942-042-1. Video. 18:00 run time. ISBN 1-55942-043-X.

Hana's Year, written by Carol Talley, illustrated by Itoko Maeno. 32 pages. ISBN 1-55942-034-0. Video. 17:10 run time. ISBN 1-55942-035-9.

Inger's Promise, written by Jami Parkison, illustrated by Andra Chase. 32 pages. ISBN 1-55942-080-4. Video. 15:00 run time. ISBN 1-55942-081-2.

Jackson's Plan, written by Linda Talley, illustrated by Andra Chase. 32 pages. ISBN 1-55942-104-5. Video. 15:00 run time. ISBN 1-55942-105-3.

Jomo and Mata, written by Alyssa Chase, illustrated by Andra Chase. 32 pages. ISBN 1-55942-051-0. Video. 20:00 run time. ISBN 1-55942-052-9.

Kiki and the Cuckoo, written by Elizabeth Happy, illustrated by Andra Chase. 32 pages. ISBN 1-55942-038-3. Video. 14:30 run time. ISBN 1-55942-039-1.

Kylie's Concert, written by Patty Sheehan, illustrated by Itoko Maeno. 32 pages. ISBN 1-55942-046-4. Video. 17:20 run time. ISBN 1-55942-047-2.

Kylie's Song, written by Patty Sheehan, illustrated by Itoko Maeno. 32 pages. (Advocacy Press) ISBN 0-911655-19-0. Video. 12:00 run time. ISBN 1-55942-021-9.

Minou, written by Mindy Bingham, illustrated by Itoko Maeno. 64 pages. (Advocacy Press) ISBN 0-911655-36-0. Video. 18:30 run time. ISBN 1-55942-015-4.

Molly's Magic, written by Penelope Colville Paine, illustrated by Itoko Maeno. 32 pages. ISBN 1-55942-068-5. Video. 16:00 run time. ISBN 1-55942-069-3.

My Way Sally, written by Mindy Bingham and Penelope Paine, illustrated by Itoko Maeno. 48 pages. (Advocacy Press) ISBN 0-911655-27-1. Video. 19:30 run time. ISBN 1-55942-017-0.

Papa Piccolo, written by Carol Talley, illustrated by Itoko Maeno. 32 pages. ISBN 1-55942-028-6. Video. 18:00 run time. ISBN 1-55942-029-4.

Pequeña the Burro, written by Jami Parkison, illustrated by Itoko Maeno. 32 pages. ISBN 1-55942-055-3. Video. 14:00 run time. ISBN 1-55942-056-1.

Plato's Journey, written by Linda Talley, illustrated by Itoko Maeno. 32 pages. ISBN 1-55942-100-2. Video. 15:00 run time. ISBN 1-55942-101-0.

Tessa on Her Own, written by Alyssa Chase, illustrated by Itoko Maeno. 32 pages. ISBN 1-55942-064-2. Video. 14:00 run time. ISBN 1-55942-065-0.

Thank You, Meiling, written by Linda Talley, illustrated by Itoko Maeno. 32 pages. ISBN 1-55942-118-5. Video. 15:00 run time. ISBN 1-55942-119-3.

Time for Horatio, written by Penelope Paine, illustrated by Itoko Maeno. 48 pages. (Advocacy Press) ISBN 0-911655-33-6. Video. 19:00 run time. ISBN 1-55942-026-X.

Tonia the Tree, written by Sandy Stryker, illustrated by Itoko Maeno. 32 pages. (Advocacy Press) ISBN 0-911655-16-6. Video. 12:10 run time. ISBN 1-55942-019-7.

You can find storybooks at better bookstores. Or you may order storybooks, videos, and activity books direct by calling MarshMedia toll free at 1-800-821-3303. MarshMedia has been publishing high-quality, award-winning learning materials for children since 1969. To receive a free catalog, call 1-800-821-3303, or visit us at www.marshmedia.com.

ANCIENT GREECE

The ancient Greeks introduced ideas that still inspire us and influence our daily lives. Their architects designed buildings that are models for our banks, libraries, and public buildings. Their artists created lifelike sculptures that are the pride of the world's art museums. The Greek epic poems *The Iliad* and *The Odyssey* are still enjoyed. Drama was invented in Athens, and plays written in ancient Greece are performed today. The Greek alphabet is the one upon which our own is based. The ancient Greeks were the first to rely on experiment and observation in conducting scientific research, and they developed basic rules of mathematics that are still used. Greek philosophers posed questions still discussed in our universities. And in the small city-states that developed in the valleys of this mountainous land, democracy had its birth.

The Parthenon
432 B.C.

Tragedy Comedy
450 B.C.

Aa Bβ Γγ Δδ Eε Zζ
Hη Θθ Iι Kκ Λλ Mμ
Nν Ξξ Oo Ππ Ρρ Σσ
Tτ Υυ Φφ Χχ Ψψ Ωω

Alphabet
900 B.C.

The Odyssey 800 B.C.

Charioteer
470 B.C.

$$a^2 + b^2 = c^2$$

Pythagorean Theorem
490 B.C.

THE ANCIENT OLYMPICS

Olympia was the site of the ancient Greek games, the model for our modern day Olympics. The games began in 776 B.C. and were held every four years. The games at Olympia were part of a religious festival in honor of Zeus, the king of Greek gods. In the beginning, the festival was a one-day event attended by people from the nearby countryside. A footrace was probably the only athletic competition. In time, the festival became a five-day affair attended by people from throughout the Greek world. The games were expanded to include a long-distance race, wrestling, boxing, chariot and horse racing, and the pentathlon. The only prize for a winner was a wreath of wild olive leaves.

During the games, a truce was observed throughout the Greek world, suspending all wars between city-states and assuring safe passage for the spectators and athletes traveling to the games. The atmosphere of the festival was much like a fair. Moving among the jostling crowds were food and drink vendors, preachers, fortune tellers, acrobats, peddlers, and politicians.

Temple of Hera
Temple of Zeus
Gymnasium

Entrance
Tunnel

Stadium

Hippodrome
(Horse Track)

Ancient Olympia